Bulldog
Your Way Through Cancer

ISBN: 9781081874094

For all the dogs of our lives. Thank you for hanging with us, for making us laugh, and for curling up with us when we're sick. Every one of you has been the best dog ever.

And for all those who are coping with cancer. If you don't have a dog to snuggle with on a bad day, curl up with this book. A good laugh is almost as helpful as a good dog.

- Beth and Josie

Foreword

When I was diagnosed with lung cancer in March 2019, one of the first things I discovered was that people wanted to help.

"If there's anything I can do, please let me know," was invariably the first thing everyone said to me – my friends, my family, local business owners like Linda, Catherine's Restaurant owner Steve and his staff (who insist on giving me a LOT of food), my mailman Kevin, my neighbors – even casual acquaintances whose names I don't know.

And they meant it. People *want* to help, but all too often we simply say thank you, and that's the end of it. So I decided from the start to give people assignments. My son Brendan is a natural for the role of Worrier in Chief, and so I assigned him that task. He's also in charge of providing me with bone marrow soup and other healthy foods and household products.

My cousins Sandy and Jane are in charge of praying. I'm not so good at that myself, but those two are formidable. Others are in charge of texting me a funny cartoon or joke each day.

Three of my grandkids – Devon, Bryce and Austin – are in charge of cheerleading. Every phone call ends with the words, "Keep on fighting, Grammy! You're going to win! I love you!" Then there is my husband Bob – my uncomplaining chief cook, grocery shopper, provider of hugs, smiles and love.

And my oldest son Sean, an oncologist – how lucky am I to have a kid who's a cancer specialist? – is in charge of making sure I have the best of doctors, infusion nurses and other professionals to take care of me. As he told me early on, "I can't drive this bus with you as the patient, but I can sit in the front seat." And he has been sitting there this whole trip.

It was an assignment to another family member that became the genesis of this book. Josie Mullally, my sons' half-sister who lives in Colorado, was among the first to ask me, "What can I do to help?"

I have seen Josie in person only twice, but I knew from her Facebook posts that she has what are quite possibly the four most adorably ugly bulldogs in all of Dogdom. And so, as a lifelong dog lover, my assignment for her was a natural.

"Send me pictures of your dogs," I told Josie. "I need to start each day with a laugh, and they're meant for the job."

And so she did. Every morning, I woke up to a wonderful new photo. (Josie apparently never sleeps – she's two time zones west of my home in New York, and she always beats me awake.) I quickly learned that Josie didn't need to start taking pictures of her dogs for me. She already had an iPhone and computer full – dogs in costumes, dogs engaged in dogly antics, dogs smiling and frowning and cuddling and sleeping and being … dogs.

"You have to realize, I'm kind of nuts," Josie confessed to me early on.

"Thank God for that!" I told her. "Because we have a book here. And we're going to call it 'Bulldog Your Way Through Cancer.'"

I told her to keep the pictures coming, and that I'd worry about the words.

By July we were done, and the book you now hold in your hands is the result of the most awesome human instinct going – wanting to do something for someone who needs a helping hand and a good laugh.

Thank you, Josie. And thank you Sophie Mullally, Mister Mullally, Einstein Mullally and Tater Tot Mullally – four outstanding members of the Mullally Nation.

And thank you to all those who continue to give me the gifts of love and laughter. I don't know how this fight will turn out, but things look promising. And with these family members, friends and dogs on my side, I have the best of all possible chances to win.

Beth Quinn
Goshen, NY
July 2019

Losing your hair?

No worries!

Put on a lovely wig ... or a fabulous scarf ... or a weird little beanie.

In fact, if ever there were a time to be weird, this is it! Who's going to criticize??!!

Well ... maybe it's possible to be a little TOO weird.

Open presents right away!

You might consider using scissors or a knife
instead of your teeth, though.
The job will go faster.

Of course, opening presents
can be pretty exhausting.

Nap time!

Best part?
YOU get to decide when ...

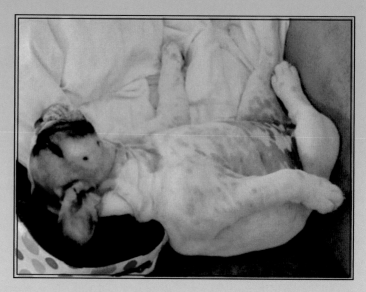

... and WHERE to take a snooze!!!
Who's gonna' argue?

Plus! You get to
wear your
all-day pajamas
and binge-watch
that show you've
been meaning
to catch up on.

OK. We get it.

You don't feel like taking a shower. Too much trouble, you say. Who's looking at you, anyway, you say.

Sure. We understand.

BUT ...

... Have you looked in the mirror lately??

Here's the thing. The better you look, the better you'll feel.

Really. We Promise.

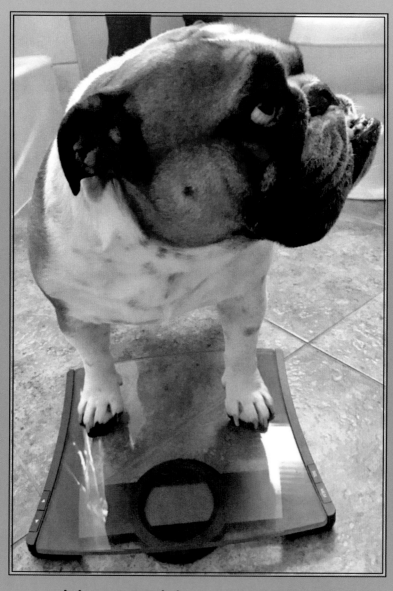

"What??? What Does it Say?
Oh no! I'm LOSING weight??!
Crazy. Usually I'm saying,
'Oh no! I'm GAINING weight!'"

Bone marrow soup?!!!
So good for the body!

And ...
whipped cream??
So good for the soul!

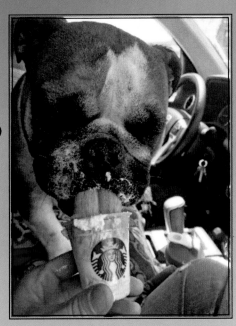

Some days it will rain ...

... and some days it will rainbow!

But when the sun

shines bright ...

... FOR CRYIN' OUT
LOUD, DON'T FORGET
the SUN SCREEN!

It's like taking that shower.
You really WILL feel better
afterward!

And you'll look better than
that dog over there, too.

(But shhhhh! Don't tell HER that!)

Feeling a little nervous
about your next
PET scan??

If so, you're not alone.
Happens to all of us.
Every time.

In fact, there's a word
for that kind of worrying.
It's called ...

Scanziety!

"I need to join a scanziety support group!
We can bite our nails together and
... ooh! I know! ...
we can have some of that medical marijuana
that calmed down the hippies!"

If someone offers
you a helping hand,

Take it!!!

And if your helper
gets a little grumpy,
try not to hear
the words.
Just hear the love
behind them.

"Look, I tolD you. It's FULL.
You go sit Down. I got this."

Need a ride home from
a chemo treatment?

Well then ... it's
probably best to call a
taxi because that
wizard just can't be
counted on!

"If only I could figure out how to tap my ruby slippers together!"

"Where IS that hot air balloon!!?!"

If you're feeling a bit confused,
it's not like you suddenly got stupid.
It's just CHEMO brain!!!
No worries. It will eventually go
away and you'll be back to being
sharp as a tack – or however
sharp you were to start with.

"I don't know, man. Is this a stick or a hot dog?"

"What IS that shiny, sparkly thing up there?! Is that a UFO or ... oh. Never mind."

It's crazy, Dude. I fell asleep a Dog and woke up an elf!"

If you have to
PUKE,
get off the couch!

This is happening to those who love you, too, ya' know.

Don't forget to give back some hugs and kisses.

Our Special Thanks To...

Einstein Mullally

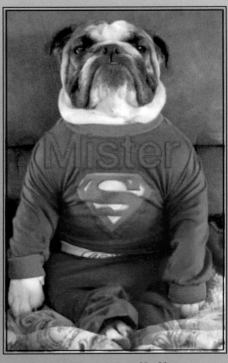

Mister Mullally

Sophie Mullally

Tater Tot Mullally

About The Photographer

*Josie Mullally with Sophie, Einstein, Mister and Tater Tot
at their home in Orchard City, Colorado.*

Josie Mullally's collection of bulldogs started when her mom insisted, after a seventeen-year battle with cancer, that she be placed in a nursing facility. Josie needed the kind of comfort in her mother's absence that only a dog (or four) can provide.

Sophie was the first. Her charming personality, along with her snaggle tooth, immediately stole Josie's heart.

Mister was the next to join the pack. He arrived on Valentine's Day in 2015, and Josie's heart was stolen again!

Einstein arrived next, as it was time to see what the smaller French bulldogs were all about. Turns out they snore louder and have a bit more gas. Who knew?

Finally, there's Tater Tot, who is comically stupid and completely uncoordinated but is the best cuddler ever.

Together they keep a smile on Josie's face and the laughter flowing. They also help Josie serve people with developmental disabilities on the Western Slope of Colorado.

If you would like to contact Josie or arrange for a book signing, she and the bulldogs can be reached at josiemullally@gmail.com.

About The Writer

Beth Quinn worked for the *Times Herald-Record* in Middletown, New York, for twenty-six years as a columnist, news and feature writer, enterprise reporter, health editor and editorial writer.

Her columns have appeared in publications ranging from the *Chicken Soup for the Soul* books and *Reader's Digest* to the *Sporting News* and *Dog Fancy*. She is also the author of *Unleashed*, a collection of her dog columns, which is available on Amazon.

She is currently an adjunct assistant professor of English at SUNY Orange. She also works with writers of both fiction and non-fiction who are interested in independent publishing and getting their work into print and for sale on Amazon. For more information about Beth's writing services, please visit bethquinnwritingservices.com.

Beth lives in Goshen, New York, with her husband Bob and their dog Scout 2.0.

Additional copies of this book are available on Amazon. To arrange a book signing (or just to chat), Beth can be reached at huckquinn@gmail.com.

Scout 2.0

PS By the way, she fully plans to beat cancer. Immunotherapy rocks! When it works, it WORKS. And it's working.